Unicorn Stories

The Unicorn and the Little Goldfish

Jan Rylewicz

Om Books International

It was too crowded in the water. Wherever Bubbles, the goldfish swam, he bumped into someone.

On his way to the fish school, he bumped into Blubber, the blue whale.

At night, the whales snored loudly above his waterbed.

He tossed and turned.

"How am I ever supposed to sleep like this?" he wondered.

The next night, Bubbles watched the bright moonlight dance above him.

He shyly poked his head out of the water.

He saw a beautiful winged horse drinking from the pond. She was covered in moonlight.

"Are you really a unicorn?" Bubbles asked.

She lifted her head, and nodded.

"Yes, I am Reema, the unicorn. I like your pretty colour. You must be a goldfish."

"It is so crowded down here," moaned Bubbles.

Reema explained that it was her fault. She wanted all the fish to get along. That's why she made even the sharks, vegetarian.

"What does that mean?" asked Bubbles.

"It means that they do not eat other fish, but it also means your pond is over-crowded," explained Reema.

The next morning, Bubbles met his friend Stormy, the shark. He didn't tell him about meeting Reema.

"Are you a vegetarian?" he asked.

"I wish I weren't," said Stormy and flashed his bright gold tooth.

"Why?" asked Bubbles.

"Because then I could eat goldfish again," grinned his friend.

From now on, Reema and Bubbles met regularly. Together they came up with a fantastic plan to make life better for all the fish and shells in the pond!

It was the weekend and there was no school for Bubbles and his friends.

The sun shone in the blue sky.

Reema put up a sign next to the water which read: ‘MOUNTAIN PLEASURE FLIGHTS.’

The plan was to take all the fish up into the air and fly them around the mountain. Up in the air the fish could forget all about being trapped in the pond.

Brave Bubbles went up first. The flight on the unicorn was an amazing experience. No goldfish had ever made it this far up in the world!

"Most goldfish have never left their aquariums. I am so lucky!" he said.

Only Stormy, the shark, looked angry. He was too scared to fly, and even the weaker fish laughed at him!

"You all wait and see!" hissed Stormy gnashing his teeth.

Bubbles flew safely inside a large water bubble on Reema's back. They flew past a family of geese. He waved at them with his fins.

"Yoo-Hoo!" he shouted, smiling.

The geese looked very surprised.

He spotted bear cubs dancing around in the snow on the mountain.

He saw Yeti, the great mountain monster. Even the Yeti waved at him!

Many other fish flew high on Reema's back that day.

They saw men and women in the market, tiny as peas. They flew through the clouds which were very cold inside. Walter, the walrus, waved at an airplane in the sky.

"Look, mummy, a flying walrus!" said a small girl inside the plane.

"Don't be silly," answered her mother.

Long after the weekend of Reema's Pleasure Flights, every fish in the pond still talked about it. The beautiful unicorn made them feel so special. They hoped that she would come back.

But Bubbles began to forget about her. As a goldfish, his memory was very poor.

He forgot all about flying, the geese and the Yeti. While the other fish dreamt of flying, Bubbles still lay awake.

Something was missing in his life.

Someone.

While he lay awake, Stormy swam up to him.

"Can't you sleep either?" asked Bubbles.

But his friend Stormy looked scary tonight, and his large gold tooth shone brightly in the moonlight.

He flashed it in front of Bubbles.

"You embarrassed me in front of everyone!" he said.

"I am sorry," apologised Bubbles. But he couldn't even remember what for.

"I am not a vegetarian anymore!" said the shark. He didn't behave like a good friend. Bubbles swam hastily to the surface to escape, but Stormy blocked his way.

"Let me through!" yelled Bubbles.

At that moment, Reema came to his rescue! She dived into the pond, and pushed Stormy away with her shining horn! She grabbed Bubbles and lifted him out of the water. He was shaking with fear.

But he finally remembered flying with Reema and felt much better.

"Everything is okay now," said Reema, touching his scales with her soft nose.

Reema finally sorted out the pond. She took the sharks back to the ocean, where they had enough space. She airlifted the octopus, the jellyfish and Walter, the walrus, back into the shallow sea waters near the coast.

Afterwards, the pond felt lovely and big.

"I should have helped a long time ago," apologised Reema, and rubbed her horn against Bubbles's button nose.

He was very thankful for such a brilliant friend.